# The Little Pioneer

# ADAM HANCHER

Doubleday Books for
Young Readers

In the fall of 1849, Papa passed on.
He left us a new homestead, but it was so far away.

"A new life!" declared Ma as we piled our belongings
into the rickety wooden wagon.

Spring had arrived, and we were
moving to California.

We gathered at
the edge of Independence,
four families all moving West.

We knew little about the trip across the Plains, but everyone had
great faith in the seasoned captain, a gruff old mountain man
by the name of Mr. Reed.

Packed, mounted, and yoked, we bid
our old life farewell.

"Westward ho!" boomed Mr. Reed, setting me to fright!

It was a fearful time in those early days,

and no doubt we all thought the same thing . . .

That our journey was to be terribly long.

My brothers soon
took to life on the prairie.
I did not.

My chores were dull and tiresome,
and I would avoid the uncultivated
Mr. Reed at all costs.

"He's a wild man!" I said to Ma.

"It helps to know wild folks when in a wild place," Ma said
as we prepared to cross the mighty Platte River.

Ma was never wrong.

That river was treacherous, swift, and swollen!

Before I knew it, the river tore me from our wagon.

Flopping and flailing, I was carried downstream,

sure I would be drowned.

But Mr. Reed, bold as ever,

plucked me from the perilous waters,

choking, soaked, and altogether shaken up.

"Thank the Lord for Mr. Reed!" Ma exclaimed.

"You owe that man an apology."

Oh, how ignorant I had been!

"Ma . . . how can I make amends?" I asked.

"You should ask Mr. Reed," she replied.

So I did.

"How can I repay you, sir?" I asked.

Mr. Reed hooted, "We'll start with this here fire—

that'll dry you out!"

With fire came toasted bread, biscuits, and buffalo stew.

Our company felt like family as we all sang to the stars.

Mr. Reed was quite at home in the wilderness, but I had much to learn.

Our old lives seemed so distant, and California felt no closer.

For months, we labored on along that dusty Emigrant Trail.

The good times passed and hardship followed.

Our wagons broke, the oxen tired,

and sickness struck us down.

Weary and footsore, we stopped to rest.

While the burdens we could no longer bear were unloaded,

I sought a shady spot to take rest.

Never had I slept so soundly as

when under that great tree.

Trouble was, when I awoke . . .

"Maaa!" I yelled with all
my might, but there was no reply.
"Mr. Reed?" I called
to no avail.

Wagon tracks scarred
the rocky landscape,
but which should I follow?
Clueless, I stumbled
deeper into the hills.

As night fell,
winter's icy fingers
slid through the trees.
Cold and alone,
I thought of Mr. Reed.
He would not despair.
He would get to work,
set up camp, and . . .

"We'll start with a fire!"
That was it.
Gathering leaves, bark,
and branches, I remembered
what I had been taught.

With flint and steel, I lit my tinder.
Sparks grew to embers, embers set
ablaze, and soon enough—

My fire roared!

Oh, how that fire lifted my spirits.
I felt safe in the warmth,
but with the fire shining
bright, I could see creatures
all around me. Mice rustled
underfoot, owls hooted
overhead, and . . . What was
that creeping toward me
out of the shadows?

A bear!

Ragged and wild, it staggered out of the darkness, fearsomely mad.

But folks must be wild in a wild place — so, cornered and panicked,

I pulled a branch from the fire. "Not now, bear!" I shouted.

"Whoa!" coughed Mr. Reed, appearing through the smoke. "I ain't no bear."

What a relief it was to see that face!

"I didn't think I'd find you, till you went an' lit that fire," he said.

"I've taken quite a liking to the wilderness," I replied.

"A real pioneer!" laughed Mr. Reed.

We woke at daybreak
and raced to the wagons.
The cold mountains
faded behind us.

The dread and fear fell away from Ma when she saw that I was safe.

Even my brothers put mischief aside to greet me.

In truth, all were in high spirits.

We had arrived in California.

Our company shared its final good-byes as we bid farewell to life on the trail.

"Westward ho!" I shouted.

Our new lives lay just over the hill . . .

. . . for us—and for Mr. Reed, too.

*To Margaret and Gary*

Copyright © 2016 by Adam Hancher
All rights reserved. Published in the United States by Doubleday, an imprint of Random House
Children's Books, a division of Penguin Random House LLC, New York. First published in hardcover
in Great Britain by Frances Lincoln Ltd., an imprint of The Quarto Group, London, in 2016.
Doubleday and the colophon are registered trademarks of Penguin Random House LLC.
Visit us on the Web! randomhousekids.com
Educators and librarians, for a variety of teaching tools, visit us at RHTeachersLibrarians.com
Library of Congress Cataloging-in-Publication Data is available upon request.
ISBN 978-1-5247-1792-6 (trade) — ISBN 978-1-5247-1793-3 (ebook)
MANUFACTURED IN CHINA
10 9 8 7 6 5 4 3 2 1
First American Edition
Random House Children's Books supports the First Amendment and celebrates the right to read.

MIX
Paper from
responsible sources
FSC® C008047
FSC
www.fsc.org